Puppy's Day Out

Based on the original screenplay, "The Pied Pupper," by M.J. Offen
Adapted by Devra Newberger Speregen

 studio fun INTERNATIONAL

When Chelsea announced to her sisters she was making a video with her puppy Honey for science class, Barbie helped her attach a mini video camera to Honey's head.

"I'm calling my video 'A Day in the Life of a Dog'!" she said. Then she turned the camera on and gave the little pup a nudge.

"OK, Honey! Go have a perfectly puppy day!"

"Let's watch on my laptop screen," Barbie said. "We can see and hear everything Honey does. And with this headset we can talk to her, too!"

"Awesome sauce!" Stacie said.

"Cool!" Skipper added. "But what's that weird crackling noise?"

Barbie pointed to Honey, who was sitting at their feet.

The girls looked down and laughed—the weird sound was just Honey scratching her neck!

"So, guess where Skipper and I are going?" Stacie asked.

"Where?" Chelsea replied.

"To *Malibu-looza*!" Stacie and Skipper cheered at the same time.

"No way!" Barbie said, excitedly. "That's an *awesome* music festival! Nikki's going there today, too! She's handing out free samples of her new health bars."

"If they're *Nikki's* new health bars, why are *you* baking them?" Skipper asked.

"Because I'm helping!" Barbie replied.

Stacie gazed around the messy kitchen. "Uh, it looks like *you're* the one who could use some help," she remarked.

"Nah, I've got this!" Barbie said confidently. "You guys go have fun at the concert!"

Later, Barbie was whipping up some more bars when Ken came over.

"Ahoy, neighbor!" Ken said cheerfully. "Ready to help me with my dance routine for the Junior Lifeguards Talent Show?"

Barbie glanced around the kitchen at all the baking she still had to do, but she didn't want to disappoint Ken. "Sure," she said. "I'll meet you by the pool."

Ken grinned. "You got it, coach!"

Barbie put the bars in the oven and headed out to the backyard.

Honey appeared in the kitchen to see what smelled so delicious! She followed the smell and jumped onto a chair, then up onto the counter.

Honey sniffed around the boxes of health bars that were ready for Nikki to pick up. But when she tried to peek into one of the boxes, she tumbled inside headfirst!

Barbie was still helping Ken when Nikki arrived to pick up the bars.

"Whoa, this box is heavy!" Nikki commented, lifting the box with Honey inside. She loaded the boxes onto her scooter and drove off.

In the backyard, Ken had fallen in the pool *twice* while trying to copy Barbie's dance moves! Finally, Barbie suggested they work on his talent show costume instead.

"Good idea!" Ken said. "I'll go home and change first."

Barbie checked the bars in the oven. She was in such a rush; she didn't notice the video playing on her laptop. If she had, she would have seen that Honey was inside a box of bars, riding on the back of Nikki's scooter!

When Nikki got to the festival, she hopped off the scooter and pulled open one of the boxes.

"Free samples!" she called out to festival-goers.

While Nikki's back was turned, the other box popped open.

Honey was happy to be in the park! A pretty butterfly flew past her face, and she jumped out of the box and raced after it!

Back at the pool, Barbie tried hard not to laugh when Ken danced around in a silly fairy costume. But she simply could not keep her giggles in when he lost his balance and fell into the pool . . . *again*!

Still laughing, Barbie helped her friend out of the pool. Suddenly, she wrinkled her nose and frowned.

"Do you smell smoke?" Barbie asked. Then she remembered the bars in the oven!

"Oh, no!" she cried as she raced back inside the house.

Barbie hurried to the kitchen. She quickly pulled out the tray of burnt bars. Then, something on her laptop screen caught her attention.

"Is that . . . *Honey*?" she said, staring at the screen in disbelief. "Chasing a butterfly . . . *at the park*?" She looked down at the counter and saw tiny paw prints in the flour.

It began to make sense.

Barbie grabbed her cell phone and called Nikki. Nikki's phone started ringing next to her on the kitchen counter.

"Nikki forgot her phone!" Barbie exclaimed.

Barbie remembered the mini video cam connected to her headset. She put in the ear buds and began calling out to Honey. "Honey, do you hear me?" she asked hopefully.

Miles away at the park, Honey stopped and looked up, searching for Barbie.

"Yes! It's me, Barbie!" Barbie cried into the headset. Honey barked and wagged her tail excitedly.

"Good girl, Honey!" Barbie said proudly. "Now, I want you to find Nikki!"

On her laptop screen, Barbie could see that Honey was looking around the park for Nikki. When the pup spotted Nikki, she barked.

"Yes! That's Nikki!" Barbie cried. "Good girl, Honey! Now go to Nikki!"

Honey took off running in Nikki's direction. But then, two pretty butterflies appeared, and Honey instantly forgot about Nikki.

"Wait! No!" Barbie called out. "No, Honey! Go to Nikki!"

But it was too late. Honey was already running after the butterflies.

Stacie and Skipper bumped into Nikki at the park.

"How's business?" Skipper asked.

"Amazing!" Nikki told her. "The bars are a HUGE hit!"

"Got any left?" Stacie chimed in. "We're starving!"

"No sweat," Nikki said, opening the second box of bars. "I have plenty—"

She peered inside the box and gasped. "It's *empty*!" she said in disbelief.

Nikki hopped on her scooter. "Tell Barbie I'm coming back for more!"

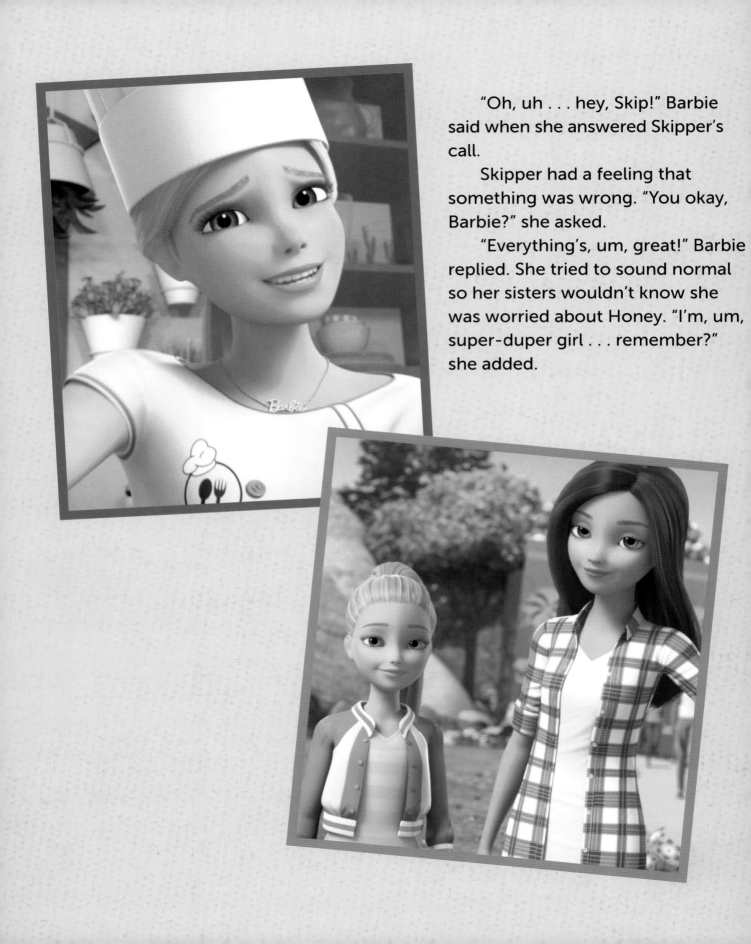

"Oh, uh . . . hey, Skip!" Barbie said when she answered Skipper's call.

Skipper had a feeling that something was wrong. "You okay, Barbie?" she asked.

"Everything's, um, great!" Barbie replied. She tried to sound normal so her sisters wouldn't know she was worried about Honey. "I'm, um, super-duper girl . . . remember?" she added.

Barbie hung up and decided to go to the park and search for Honey. She grabbed Nikki's phone, a fresh box of bars, and hopped in her car.

On the way there, Barbie saw Nikki coming from the park. She signaled for Nikki to pull over.

"Here's your phone and some more bars! Bye!" Barbie said. She quickly handed everything to Nikki, then jumped back in her car.

In the park, Barbie found Honey chasing butterflies.

"Come here, girl!" Barbie called out as she raced after the puppy.

Stacie and Skipper were heading back to the concert when they saw a puppy that looked like Honey race past them.

"Wait, that *is* Honey!" Stacie exclaimed. "And that's definitely Barbie chasing after her!"

Barbie stopped to catch her breath. She saw Honey follow the butterfly to the foot of a large tree that had a ladder leaning against it.

Before Barbie could catch her, Honey scampered up the ladder! She followed the butterfly up the tree, to the edge of a very high branch. Honey was stuck in the tree!

Barbie ran to the tree and carefully climbed to where Honey was stuck. Barbie coaxed her as gently as she could. Honey crept slowly back along the branch toward Barbie. "That's it, Honey! C'mon girl!" she said softly.

Finally, Honey jumped into her arm

Barbie breathed a sigh of relief and hugged the pup tightly.

Honey was so happy, she licked Barbie's face all over, causing Barbie to lose her balance!

But Barbie, always the gymnast, wa able to catch the branch with her knee and save both of them from falling!

Stacie, Skipper, and Nikki arrived to find Barbie and Honey hanging upside-down from the branch—without a way down. The ladder that had been leaning against the tree was gone!

"So, would *now* be a good time to offer you our help?" Skipper called up to her big sister.

"Yes, please!" Barbie laughed.

Stacie spotted a park worker with a ladder and called him over. Soon, both Barbie and Honey were safe on the ground.

A few days later, Chelsea played her video for everyone.

"This is my favorite part!" she chuckled. The part where Honey licks Barbie's face and the two of them lose their balance and hang from the tree played, and everyone laughed.

"I really wanted to help *everyone*," Barbie told her sisters and friends. "But I was the one who ended up needing help!"

"Everyone needs help sometimes," Stacie said, giving her big sister a hug.

Barbie held her arms out for everybody else to join in. "Come on! Bring it in, guys!"

Smiling and laughing, Skipper, Chelsea, Nikki, and Ken joined the hug.